Jump aboard the tractor and count as you ride,
All the different animals in the countryside.

Chug, chug, chug.

Stop the tractor for **one** hungry cow.

Farmer Tom has finished working for the day,
He's fed all the animals and cut down all the hay.

Chug, chug, chug.

Stop the tractor for **two** whinnying horses.

Farmer Tom is driving the tractor back to the barn,
Collecting the animals, to keep them safe from harm.

Chug, chug, chug.

Stop the tractor for **three** fluffy sheep.

Past fields of maize and barley the tractor chugs on by,
As the sun shines down brightly, from the clear blue sky.

Chug, chug, chug.

Stop the tractor for **four** excitable dogs.

The rickety tractor trailer is really tightly packed,
But more animals are waiting, to clamber on the back.

Chug, chug, chug.

MIAOW!

MIAOW!

Stop the tractor for **five** playful cats.

As the tractor passes fields, all brown and freshly ploughed,
The farm animals are making the most horrendous sound!

Chug, chug, chug.

Stop the tractor for a gaggle of SIX geese.

The sunlight is fading as the barn comes into sight,
A hungry owl leaves her nest as day turns into night.

Chug, chug, chug.

Stop the tractor for **seven** fidgety piglets.

Farmer Tom drives his tractor around the farm all day.
Who else will join this happy band, before they drive away?

Chug, chug, chug.

Stop the tractor for **eight** smelly goats.

Although it's near the very end of a very busy day,
The energetic animals still want to have fun and play!

Chug, chug, chug.

Stop the tractor for **nine** brown hens.

Now it's time for bed, so why don't you look,
And count up all the animals you met in this book?

Chug, chug, chug.

EEK! EEK!
EEK!
EEK!
EEK!
EEK!
EEK!
EEK!

Stop the tractor for **ten** field mice.

The End